Postman Pat's
Places

Hippo

Scholastic Children's Books,
Commonwealth House, 1-19 New Oxford Street,
London WC1A 1NU, UK
a division of Scholastic Ltd

London ~ New York ~ Toronto ~ Sydney ~ Auckland

First published by Scholastic Ltd, 1998

ISBN 0 590 19541 7

Printed in Belgium

This is Greendale Post Office.
"Good morning, Mrs Goggins!" says
Postman Pat.

Inside the Post Office, Mrs Goggins and
Pat sort out the letters and parcels.

Sometimes, Postman Pat and Jess deliver
letters to Ted Glen's workshop.

Doctor Gilbertson leaves her surgery to visit her patients.

Pat has a delivery for Reverend Timms
at St Thomas's Church.

Inside the church, Pat and Reverend Timms talk about the next choir practice.

Sometimes Pat rides a bicycle round
Greendale to deliver the post.
Jess sits in the front basket.

Pat and Jess visit George Lancaster at
Intake Farm on his birthday.
"Ooh, a parcel!" says George, "How exciting!"

Postman Pat watches Alf Thompson
carefully drive his tractor through the
gates at Thompson Ground.

Every day, Postman Pat and Jess visit
all the corners of Greendale to
collect the post.

Pat delivers a parcel to Garner Hall.
"Anybody home?" calls Pat.

Major Forbes is having the roof fixed
at Garner Hall.

Pat helps Dorothy Thompson carry a ladder at Thompson Ground.

At the end of each day, Postman Pat and Jess drive past all their favourite places in Greendale.